-THE CHRONICLES OF-
NARNIA
PRINCE CASPIAN
Caspian's Army

Adapted by Sadie Chesterfield
Illustrated by Justin Sweet
Based on the screenplay by Andrew Adamson & Christopher Markus & Stephen McFeely
Based on the book by C. S. Lewis

HarperEntertainment
An Imprint of HarperCollinsPublishers

Prince Caspian: Caspian's Army
Copyright © 2008 by C.S. Lewis Pte. Ltd.
Art/illustration © 2008 Disney Enterprises, Inc. and Walden Media, LLC.
Printed in the United States of America.

Library of Congress catalog card number: 2007942257
ISBN 978-0-06-123157-5

Typography by Rick Farley
❖
First Edition

PROLOGUE

A long time ago, four children discovered a magical land called Narnia. The creatures of Narnia loved them, and the children were soon crowned Kings and Queens. They ruled in peace until the day they disappeared.

Now Narnia is ruled by an evil Telmarine King named Miraz. He stole the throne from his nephew, Prince Caspian. When Miraz's Telmarine soldiers first invaded the forest, many creatures were killed. So many that Miraz's people now believe Narnians are extinct. But some are still hiding, waiting for someone to come and lead them to freedom.

Night falls in Narnia. A young Prince named Caspian races through the thick forest on horseback. Soldiers chase him, their swords ready to strike.

Caspian dodges through the trees until he can no longer hear the soldiers' shouts. He glances behind him and sees . . . nothing. Has he really lost them?

WHACK! With his head turned, Caspian slams into a thick tree branch and gets thrown from his horse. He is knocked out cold.

Caspian awakes in a strange place. Tree roots crisscross the low ceiling. He feels a bandage on his head.

Caspian can hear voices in the next room. He gets up and moves to the doorway to listen.

"You said you would get rid of him!" a gruff voice yells.

"We can't kill him *now*," a quiet voice replies. "I just bandaged his head—he's a guest!"

A large Badger enters the room, holding a bowl of soup. He's followed
by a Dwarf with a black beard. Caspian jumps back in shock.
"You're Narnians," he gasps. "You're supposed to be extinct."

The creatures introduce themselves as Trufflehunter the Badger and Nikabrik the Dwarf.

They think Caspian is one of King Miraz's soldiers.

"I'm not a soldier. I'm Prince Caspian, the tenth of that name," he explains. "My uncle stole my throne, so I'm running away. I have to go—Miraz's soldiers won't stop chasing me until I'm dead."

"You can't leave," Trufflehunter cries, pointing to a small ivory horn hanging from Caspian's waist. "Don't you know what that is?"

Caspian shrugs. The horn was a gift
from a friend.

"You're meant to save us," Trufflehunter
says. "It is said that whoever blows it will
lead us to freedom."

But Caspian has no time to talk. He knows
the soldiers are still searching for him.

"Run!" he shouts, as soldiers emerge from behind the trees.
Arrows whiz past Caspian's head and one finds a target.
Trufflehunter is wounded!
The brave Badger tells Caspian to leave him behind.

Caspian knows he has to help his new friend.
He hoists the Badger over his shoulder and runs as fast as he can.
The soldiers are still chasing him—one is right at his heels.

Just then, the soldier falls. Another soldier falls, then another, until the wood is silent.

Then a Mouse appears—the biggest Mouse Caspian has ever seen. He approaches Caspian, his sword drawn.

"Reepicheep, stay your blade!" Trufflehunter shouts.

Caspian holds up the horn and the Mouse's eyes widen.

"Bring it forward," says a deep voice. A Centaur named Glenstorm steps out from behind a tree. "This is the reason we've gathered," he says.

The Centaur leads the Narnians to a clearing in the wood. Caspian looks around him at the Fauns, Centaurs, Squirrels and Mice he has only heard about in bedtime stories. All the Narnians have come out from hiding. Everything is about to change.

The creatures surround Caspian and begin to shout. After years of fighting Miraz's soldiers, they do not trust humans. "Murderer!" they cry. "Kill him!"

"Shall we list the things humans have taken from us?" asks a Centaur.
"Our homes!" yells a Faun.
"Our freedom!" adds a Gryphon.

"I can help you!" Caspian shouts. "The throne is rightfully mine. Help me claim it, and I can bring peace between us."

A Squirrel steps forward.

"Do you really think there can be peace?" he asks.

Caspian smiles. "Whether this horn is magic or not, it brought us together. And together we have a chance to take back what is ours."

The Faun looks to the Gryphon, who looks to the Mice below him. Slowly, everyone agrees. Working together they will fight Miraz and his soldiers. They are an army now. They will take back Narnia!